Fran and Gran

Written by
Stacey Chaikin
Illustrated by
Aura Moser

115 Bluebill Drive
Savannah, GA 31419
United States

Copyright © 2012 Stacey Chaikin
Edited by Kimberly Feltes Taylor
Printed and bound in the United States of America
First printing 2013

ISBN 978-1-60131-100-9

Published with the assistance of the helpful folks at DragonPencil.com

For Granny Rose, who gave me wonderful memories and with lots of love to my six sweetpeas . . .

Grace
Charlie
CeCe
Riley
Kitty
and
Micah

. . . who give me more joy and love than I could ever imagine.
XOXO,
Nana

KNOCK! KNOCK! KNOCK! Gran was at the door. "Ready for our trip?" she asked.

"No," Fran whispered. She had never been away from home.

"We'll see the Liberty Bell," Gran said.

Still, Fran wasn't tempted.

"We'll visit the Badlands," Gran said.

"Really?" Fran asked, her curiosity piqued.

"We'll even ride horses," Gran promised.

"Okay!"

So off went Fran and Gran on a cross-country adventure!

CLANG! BANG! Crank! **HONK!** Fran and Gran were in New York City. The buildings reached up to the clouds. The cars zoomed down the streets. The people hurried from one place to another.

Fran and Gran hurried, too.

Finally, they found the bus station.

"Oh, my!" said Fran, as she stepped aboard the bus. It was full of Trailblazers. They were shouting. They were playing games. They were jumping up and down.

Gran took no notice of the boys and settled into her seat.

But Fran had never been in the midst of such chaos. And when the Trailblazers all turned to stare at her, all she could do was stare back.

Whoosh! The bus door closed. Vrooom! The engine started up. Fran and Gran were on their way!

"This is the Continental Express!" the bus driver announced.

"Woo Hoo!" cheered the Trailblazers.

"Woo . . . hoo . . . ," Fran squeaked.

"Ahhhhhhh," Gran yawned before dozing off.

"Next stop, Philadelphia!" the bus driver said.

Fran and Gran went right to the Liberty Bell.

"Let's get a better look," said Gran, stepping closer and closer. Until . . . she tripped and fell right onto the Liberty Bell!

"Gran! You cracked it!" Fran shouted.

"Let's go!" Gran said.

"You cracked the Liberty Bell!" Fran said again.

But Gran just stormed back to the bus. And Fran couldn't help but let out a giggle.

"**_ZZZZZZZ! Zzzzzz. ZZZZZZZ_**!" snored Gran, as the bus came to a stop.

"Gran, wake up!" Fran said. "We're at the car museum!"

Fran ran from car to car, stopping at a bright blue one. "Can we get in?" Fran pestered Gran.

Gran peered to her right. She peered to her left. No one was watching. "Well, just for a minute," she whispered.

Before Fran knew it, they had lurched out the front door and were headed downtown.

All the people cheered! All the cars honked! They had never seen such an unusual sight.

Gran smiled widely. Fran waved to the crowd.

Suddenly, a police officer jumped in front of them. "Halt!" she ordered.

Gran's face turned bright red.

And Fran couldn't help but let out a giggle.

Strum·a·lum, strum·a·loo. Strum·a·lum . . . . Fran peered out the window. "Gran! Look!" she said.

"This must be Memphis!" Gran howled. "Let me put on my blue suede shoes!"

"Huh?" said Fran.

But Gran simply grabbed Fran's hand and pulled her off the bus.

"Where are we going?" asked Fran.

"Graceland!" Gran said.

At the museum, Gran peered to her right. She peered to her left. "No one is watching," Gran whispered.

Next thing Fran knew, Gran was clad in a red jumpsuit. So Fran shimmied into a white one.

"Well, it's one for the money . . . ," Gran sang.

"Two for the show . . . ," Fran chimed in.

"Out!" the manager of Graceland shouted.

And Fran couldn't help but let out a giggle.

Bumpity bump. Bumpity bump. Bumpity bump.
BUMP! Fran woke to find Gran standing in the aisle, quite upset.

"I cannod bind my deeph!" Gran whispered.

"What?" Fran asked.

Gran smiled a big, toothless smile.

"Ohhhh!" Fran jumped up. "You cannot find your teeth!"

"I CANNOD BIND MY DEEPH!" Gran shouted to the whole bus.

The Trailblazers awoke at once. "What? What did she say?" they grumbled.

"She cannot find her teeth," Fran answered as sweetly as she could.

Screeeecccchhhh! The driver stopped the bus.

The Trailblazers looked under their seats. They looked in their bags. They searched everywhere for Gran's missing teeth.

"I found them!" one Trailblazer called from the back.

Soon, the bus was on its way again.

And Fran couldn't help but let out a giggle.

CREAK! ~~Hiss!~~ *Ssswwwishhh* . . . "What's that?" Fran asked nervously.

"Just some trouble getting up these mountain roads," the bus driver said.

Soon, the bus ground to a halt.

Gran saw a sign: Welcome to the Cave State! "Well, I've never been in a cave!" Gran proclaimed.

"Now's your chance," the bus driver said. So Gran, Fran, and the Trailblazers headed into a cave. With each step, the cave got darker and darker and darker.

"Which way?" Fran whispered to Gran.

"To the right," Gran whispered back.

"I don't think we're still with the group," Fran whispered.

"Indeed, we are." Gran pulled out a match. "See," she said as she lit the match, "we're still . . . ."

"EEEEKKKKKK!" Gran screamed.

"EEEEEKKKKKKK!" Fran screamed.

"*Screeeecccchhhh!*" screamed all the bats!

Fran and Gran turned and ran all the way back to the bus.

"I am never going in a cave again!" Gran huffed as she settled into her seat.

And Fran couldn't help but let out a giggle.

Click, *clack*. Click, *clack*. Click, *clack*.
Gran knit row upon row, quickly turning a ball of yarn into a beautiful scarf. Fran was intrigued.

"Would you like to try?" asked Gran.

"Indeed, I would," said Fran.

So Gran handed Fran her own set of needles and a great big ball of pink yarn. Soon, Fran's and Gran's needles click-clacked in unison.

In just a few hours, Fran knit a hat.

Gran knit a sweater.

Fran knit a pair of mittens.

Gran knit a pair of booties. She even knit an umbrella!

And Fran couldn't help but let out a giggle.

Woooooosh! A slap of wind met Fran and Gran at the Badlands.

"Look at the buffalo, Fran," Gran said. "Look at the prairie dogs. Look at the . . . ."

Another slap of wind knocked Gran off the cliff. She rolled down and down. "Frannnnnn!" Gran called.

Later, at Mount Rushmore, Gran ignored everyone who stared at her dusty layer. She even got someone to take their picture. Fran knew it would be a moment to remember.

And she couldn't help but let out a giggle.

SLAM! The heavy door shut tightly behind them.

"Uh-oh," Gran said.

"Ooooh!" Fran gasped.

Dozens of curious faces stared up at them.

"The bus . . . ," Gran started.

". . . it got us here late," Fran squeaked. Then she turned bright red.

"It's my mother and my niece," the professor announced. "Come down here. Take a front seat."

So Gran led the way, smiling and waving to all the students. Fran tip-toed behind her, wishing she could become invisible.

Soon after they settled into their seats, Fran heard a strange sound. "Could it be?" Fran thought. She turned to Gran. Sure enough, Gran was snoring through the lecture.

And Fran couldn't help but let out a giggle.

Clop! Clop! Clop! Fran was riding a brown filly. Gran was planted on a silver mare called Pokey.

Suddenly, Pokey stopped. Gran shook the reins. She tapped her toes. But Pokey wouldn't budge.

"Move along!" a ranch hand finally yelled at Pokey.

She let out a "Neigh!"

Then she galloped away.

"Frannnnnnnn!" Gran yelled, bouncing left and right. "I'm never riding a horse againnnnnnn!"

And Fran couldn't help but let out a giggle.

Aaachooooo! "What was that?" Fran asked, her eyes opening wide.

"Just the bus driver," Gran whispered. "He sneezed. Now, go back to sleep."

But Fran couldn't sleep. "Tell me a story," she begged.

"Well," started Gran, "when I was your age, I went on a long trip, too."

"Where did you go?"

"I came to America."

"Where did you come from?"

"Poland."

"Why did you leave?" Fran asked.

"Life in Poland was hard," Gran said. "My father couldn't find a job. We didn't have any money. We didn't have any food. If we had stayed, we could have starved to death."

"Oh, no!" Fran said.

"But not to worry," Gran said. "My father got us to America. He found a job. He worked hard. We had plenty of food. Life was good for us. And now, not so many years later, I am able to see this great country with you."

And Fran couldn't help but let a tear roll down her cheek.

ScreeEEcccchhhh! The bus stopped. "Time for a swim," Gran said.

Soon, Gran was in the water. Fran stood tentatively on shore.

"You can't sink in Salt Lake, Fran. It's too salty," said Gran. "See how easily I float . . . ."

Suddenly, a wave knocked into Gran. It spun her around and around. She tried to stand up, to no avail. "Frannnnnn!" Gran called.

Fran jumped into the water. She swam to Gran. She pulled. She prodded. But try as she might, Fran could not put Gran upright.

Then the Trailblazers rushed to Gran. They pushed. They pulled. They prodded, too. Soon they had Gran back on her feet.

"I'm never going swimming again!" Gran huffed, as she stormed back to the bus.

And Fran couldn't help but let out a giggle.

FLUMP! Clink! *Fizz* . . . . Fran's race car came to a halt. "Hmmmm," Fran said. "My car won't go!"

Soon, one car, then another, lined up behind Fran. And she turned bright red.

A mechanic tinkered with Fran's car. Still, it wouldn't go.

"I'll just have to get out," said Fran. But she couldn't move. "The steering wheel dropped down! I'm stuck!"

So the attendant pushed. She pulled. But there was no getting Fran out of that car.

"I know," the attendant finally said. She pulled out her wrench and yanked out the steering wheel. Then she yanked Fran out, too.

"Back to the bus!" Fran said.

And this time, Gran couldn't help but let out a giggle.

After two weeks of fun, Fran and Gran were heading home—by plane.

"Next time, Europe!" Gran said. "I've always wanted to ski in Switzerland!"

And Fran couldn't help but let out a giggle.